W9-BQI-378

OCT 1976
RECEIVED
OHIO DOMINICAN
COLLEGE LIBRARY
COLUMBUS, OHIO
43219

OHIO DOMINICAN COLLEGE LIBRARY
COLUMBUS, OHIO 43219

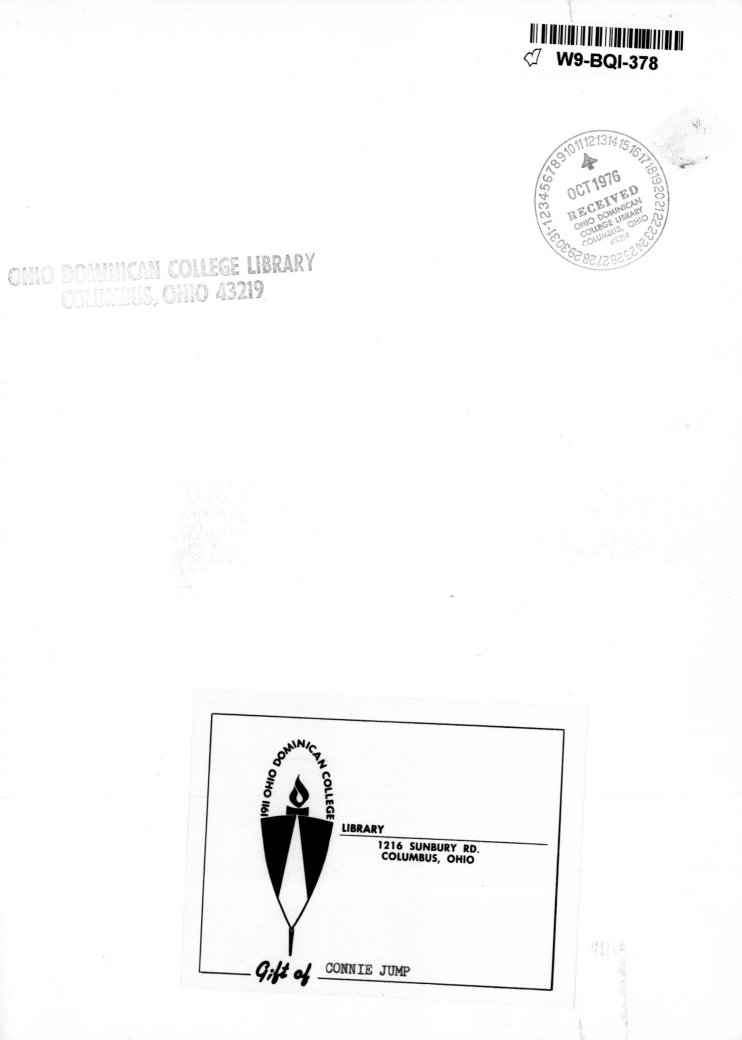

1961 OHIO DOMINICAN COLLEGE

LIBRARY
1216 SUNBURY RD.
COLUMBUS, OHIO

Gift of CONNIE JUMP

J
W

Library of Congress Cataloging in Publication Data

Wildsmith, Brian.
    Brian Wildsmith, Maurice Maeterlinck's Blue
bird.

    SUMMARY: Using art based on designs for
the film, *The Blue Bird*, the author recounts his ver-
sion of two children's search for the bluebird of
happiness.
    [1. Fantasy] I. Maeterlinck, Maurice, 1862—
1949. L'oiseau bleu. II. Title.
PZ7.W647Bs   [E]   76—16541
ISBN 0—531—02476—8
ISBN 0—531—00352—3 lib. bdg.

Originating publisher
Oxford University Press, London

All rights reserved
Printed in the United States of America
6   5   4   3   2   1

Brian Wildsmith:

Maurice Maeterlinck's
Blue Bird

FRANKLIN WATTS | NEW YORK | LONDON | 1976

Text copyright © 1976 by Brian Wildsmith from
the play *The Blue Bird* by Maurice Maeterlinck

Illustrations copyright © 1976 by Wenles Films,
Ltd. and Brian Wildsmith

99818

Deep in the heart of a forest, the evening sun was setting. All that could be heard was the twittering of birds and the soft rustle of leaves and undergrowth as the animals went to their homes and their young.

99818

Two children, called Mytyl and Tyltyl, were asleep in a woodcutter's cottage. They dreamed of a wonderful party, with mountains of cakes to eat and oceans of lemonade to drink.

Suddenly the bedroom door creaked open, and there stood an old lady in a red cloak and hood.

"Mrs. Berlingot?" Mytyl sat up and rubbed her eyes. "What are you doing here?"

"I am not your neighbor Mrs. Berlingot!" the old woman snapped. "I'm the fairy Bérylune. Have you the bird that is blue?"

"Only my little blue bird," Tyltyl replied.

"I've seen that bird," said the fairy. "It's not blue enough.

My little girl is ill and
very, very unhappy.
Only the Blue Bird
will make her happy.

"Will you help
me look for the Blue
Bird?" said Bérylune.
"I can't do it all by
myself."

"Yes, yes, of
course we will," cried
Mytyl and Tyltyl.

"Then you must
get dressed. Tyltyl,
wear this magic hat
with the diamond."

Tyltyl put the hat
on. "It isn't magic!"
he said. "I still feel
the same."

"Turn the
diamond. Turn the
diamond and you
will see," replied
Bérylune.

Tyltyl turned the diamond. Bérylune became a wonderful beauty. The walls of their home gleamed and sparkled like precious stones.

"How wonderful," the children cried. "I never knew our house was so beautiful."

"That is because you never really saw it. The diamond helps you see things as they really are," said the fairy.

With that the clock chimed, and out tumbled twenty-four little men. They laughed and danced all over the table before they dashed back into the clock.

"Who are they?" asked Tyltyl, amazed.

"They are the hours of your day, waiting for you to fill them with happiness or sadness," replied the fairy.

Just then the faucet began singing in a very high voice. Water streamed from it and changed into a lady with a flowing headdress of water flowers.

"Who is she?" asked Tyltyl. "She'll catch cold—she's all wet."

"Ah! That is the soul of Water." The fairy smiled. "She doesn't mind being wet."

Then the milk jug wobbled and jobbled and fell on its side, spilling the milk on the table. A figure, white and shy, arose. She began mopping up the milk with her dress.

"That's Milk. She's shy and confused because she spilt the milk," exclaimed the fairy.

Next a funny little man covered with candies rose out of the sugar bowl. He had a big smile on his face.

"I think you must be Sugar," said Mytyl.

"Quite right, my dear. What a charming girl! Would you like a candy?" he asked, as he plucked one off his smock and offered it to her.

Just then a stoutish gentleman stepped out of the bread bowl. He patted and pushed at himself as he tried to tighten his belt. "It's no good! I'm just too fat. I must stop eating so much yeast. Hello," he cried. "Bread's the name. Here, try some." And he plucked a bun from behind his head.

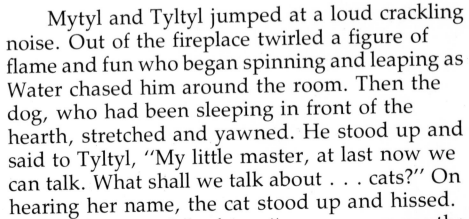

Mytyl and Tyltyl jumped at a loud crackling
noise. Out of the fireplace twirled a figure of
flame and fun who began spinning and leaping as
Water chased him around the room. Then the
dog, who had been sleeping in front of the
hearth, stretched and yawned. He stood up and
said to Tyltyl, "My little master, at last now we
can talk. What shall we talk about . . . cats?" On
hearing her name, the cat stood up and hissed.

"There," said the fairy, "now you can see the
souls of Cat and Dog."

Fire, Water, Sugar, Bread, Milk, Cat, and Dog all crowded around the two children. "Why aren't you in bed?" they asked.

"We have to look for the Blue Bird. Will you help us?" said Tyltyl.

"Of course we will. But where must we go to find the Blue Bird?" they all cried.

"First we will travel through the mists of time. Then Mytyl and Tyltyl must go alone to the Land of Memory. Perhaps they will find the Blue Bird there," the fairy said.

24

After traveling a long way, Mytyl and Tyltyl came to the Land of Memory. When the mist cleared, they saw their grandparents.

"I thought we'd see you today," said Grandpa, smiling and clapping. "My left foot was itching!"

"We miss you very much, you know," said Mytyl. "Are you still dead?"

"You have only to think of us and we come alive," said Grandma, hugging them.

"Can you help us find the Blue Bird?" asked Tyltyl.

"How sad," said Grandpa. "He's not here. We have no Blue Bird."

25

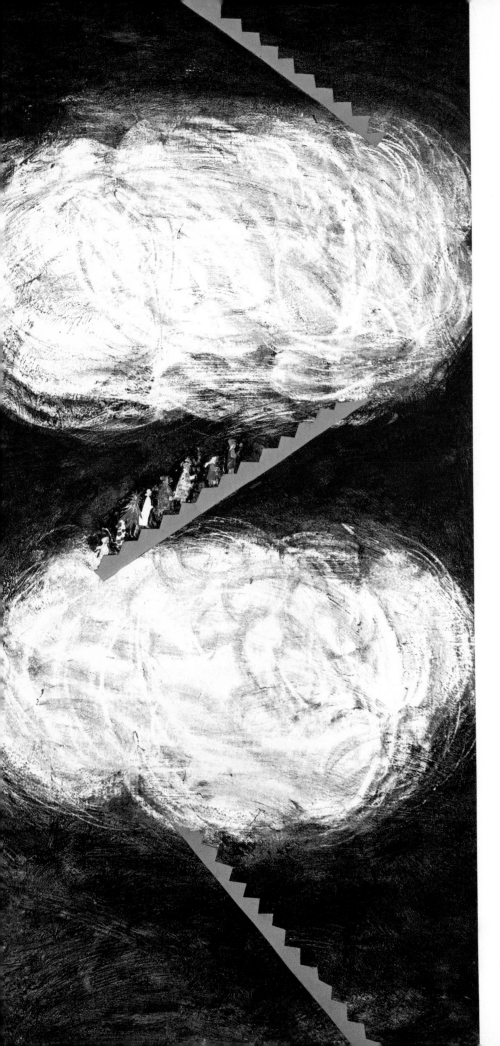

Tyltyl and Mytyl kissed their grandparents good-bye. As they came back out of the mists of time, the fairy Bérylune, Bread, Sugar, Milk, Water, Fire, Cat, and Dog were waiting for them.

"Did you find the Blue Bird?" they cried.

"No," said Tyltyl in a quiet voice. "The Blue Bird wasn't there."

"Then you must go to the Palace of Night," said the fairy. "It will be a perilous journey, for the palace is high in the sky. Come, I will lead you to the cloud steps.

"I cannot come with you into the Palace of Night," the fairy said. "Only darkness is allowed, and I am full of light. Mrs. Night guards the palace. She has all the keys to the secret rooms. But she cannot refuse you a key if you ask for it."

The children climbed the cloud steps and
wearily entered the great hall of the Palace of
Night.

"Good day, Mrs. Night," said Tyltyl.

"Good day!!! You may say 'good night' or
'good evening,' but not 'good day,' " she replied.

"I beg your pardon, Mrs. Night, but we are
looking for the Blue Bird."

"He is not here," she said.

"Give me your keys to the secret rooms. I
must search them," said Tyltyl.

Finally, the children found the first room. It was full of all the ghosts of the past. The second was full of all the sickness in the world. The third held the terrors of the world, and the fourth contained all the world's mysteries. But there was no Blue Bird.

The fifth room left them dazzled and bewildered. It was the garden of dreams. "We've found it!" cried Tyltyl. "It's full of Blue Birds. They are eating the moonbeams. Look, they fly into my hands."

They filled the cage they had brought and hurried out into daylight. But when they reached the fairy, all the birds were dead.

"Do not cry, children. Those were night birds. You did not catch the one able to live in daylight. Hurry, we must try the forest," said the fairy.

28

As the children entered the forest, Tyltyl
spoke to the trees. There was a rustling of leaves,
and the trees opened to make way for the soul
that each one contained. Tyltyl spoke to the Oak,
the Cypress, the Lime, and the Willow, but they
did not have the Blue Bird.

"Go away," they cried. "You are our enemy.
You cut off our arms and heads to make fires,
houses, and tables! Go away, we will not help
you."

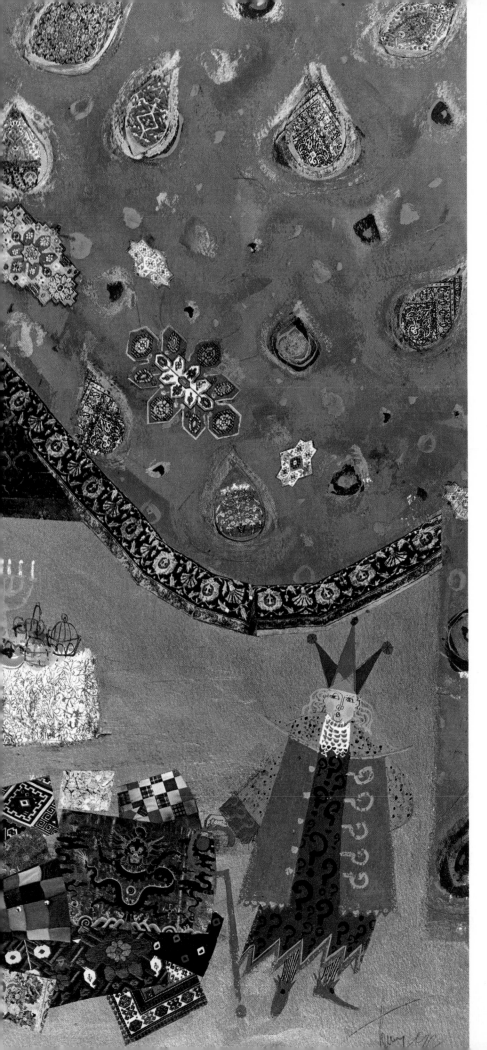

The fairy was very disappointed, but she took the children to the Palace of Luxuries. Perhaps they would find the Blue Bird there.

The Luxuries of the world sat eating, drinking, shouting, sleeping, and singing together.

Mytyl and Tyltyl gorged themselves with delightful food while they watched a wonderful circus. Beside them stood the Luxury of Knowing Nothing. He watched the circus, but didn't understand it.

"How silly this place is," said Tyltyl. "The Blue Bird isn't here—let's turn the diamond and find the fairy."

33

Disappointed again, the fairy took them to
the Palace of the Future. "We are now at the
celestial palace," she said. "You are in the midst
of children who are not yet born."

"How splendid it all is!" said Tyltyl. As he
spoke, all the unborn children came running up
to see them.

"Live children, come and look at the live
children!" they cried.

"Why do they call us live children?" asked Mytyl.

"Because they themselves are awaiting the hour of their birth," replied the fairy. "Come in, we don't have much time."

As they entered the palace halls, the fairy explained that all the unborn children were building a future for themselves. "There is a librarian. There is an engineer. That one will be a plumber. Over there, a way to explore the stars is being invented. There is a machine that will dig to the center of the earth. That one will heat the cold regions of our planet." The fairy looked about. "I see no Blue Bird," she said sadly. "We have failed. There is nowhere else to look."

The dispirited group arrived at the cottage.
Mytyl and Tyltyl said tearful good-byes to the
fairy and then to Cat, Dog, Bread, Milk, Water,
Fire, and Sugar. As the fairy turned the diamond,
they all quietly took their original form. Sugar and
Bread went to their places on the table. Milk
turned up the fallen jug and slid into it. Water
flowed into the dripping faucet, and Fire sank
into the dying embers on the hearth. Cat and Dog
fell asleep in front of the fire.

The children climbed into bed and went to
sleep. At dawn they awoke. They were still
wearing their day clothes. "Then we did go
through the mists of time," Mytyl cried. "We saw
all those strange and wondrous things!"

Once downstairs, they danced around the room, to the surprise of their parents. Suddenly Mytyl pointed to her bird. "Oh!" she said. "He is blue! He is much bluer than he was last night."

"It's the Blue Bird we've been looking for. He was here all the time," shouted Tyltyl.

Some time later their neighbor, Mrs. Berlingot, arrived at the cottage. "I'm so happy!" she exclaimed. "My little girl is well! She can walk, run, and dance."

Outside, the three children admired the Blue Bird. "There are bluer ones," said Tyltyl, "but you can't catch them."

"That doesn't matter," replied the little girl. "He's beautiful. May I hold him?" she asked.

"Of course," said Tyltyl happily. But as he took the bird from the cage, the bird escaped and flew away.

"He's gone," sobbed the little girl. "He's gone."

Tyltyl watched the bird disappear into the clouds and, with a mixture of happiness and sadness, said, "I know, but I'll catch another one for you."

99818

DATE DUE

FEB 14 '7	FEB 6 '8		
MAR 28 '77	FEB 14 '85		
APR 19 '77	MAY 11 '86		
AUG 05 '7	FEB 12 '87		
NOV 22 '7	FEB 2 0 1990		
MAR 1 '79	AUG 0 9 1990		
APR 0 5 '79			
OCT 2 '79			
OCT 0 7 '80			
FEB 19 1983			
DEC 1 0 1983			
DEC 1 0 1983			

J
W
Wildsmith, Brian
Maurice Maeterlinck's Blue bird.

Ohio Dominican College Library
1216 Sunbury Road
Columbus, Ohio 43219

DEMCO